SUPER FLYERS

Neil Francis

ILLUSTRATIONS BY
June Bradford

Addison-Wesley Publishing Company, Inc.
Reading, Massachusetts   Menlo Park, California   New York
Don Mills, Ontario   Wokingham, England   Amsterdam
Bonn   Sydney   Singapore   Tokyo   Madrid   San Juan

First published in Canada in 1988 by Kids Can Press,
Toronto, Ontario.

First published in the U.S. in 1988 by Addison-Wesley
Publishing Company, Inc., Reading, Massachusetts.

Library of Congress Cataloging-in-Publication Data
Francis, Neil.
 Super flyers/by Neil Francis; illustrated by June Bradford.
 p. cm.
 Summary: Provides instructions on how to make and fly
a variety of flying craft, including paper airplanes, dirigibles, parachutes, and kites.
 ISBN 0-201-14933-8
 1. Paper airplanes—Juvenile literature. 2. Kites—Juvenile
literature. I. Bradford, June, ill. II. Title.
 [DNLM: 1. Paper airplanes. 2. Kites. 3. Handicraft.]
TL770.F56 1988   88-19336
745.592—dc19

Edited by Valerie Wyatt
Cover artwork by June Bradford
Cover design by Copenhaver Cumpston
Book design by Michael Solomon
Set in 12-point Administer Book by Compeer Typographic
Services Limited

BCDEFGHIJ—VB—898
Second Printing, October 1988

Contents

Flying Super Flyers

This book shows you a lot of really great flying machines you can make and fly. And it tells you how they (and real flyers such as airplanes and helicopters) get and stay airborne.

If you think you've seen some of these designs before, look again. Even the planes that seem familiar have a new twist to them. And there's also info on how to do some amazing test pilot experiments and aerobatics.

Designs for paper airplanes and other flyers are very local. Each region has its own favourites, and these are passed from kid to kid. Some of the flyers you find in this book come from my schooldays in the 1930s at Balmy Beach School in Toronto. Later, as I travelled around as an Air Force pilot, I saw these same designs, with local variations, all across the country.

Have fun trying these designs, and then start fiddling and see if you can come up with modifications that make them fly even better. Happy flying!

Neil Francis
Carp, Ontario
1988

GLIDERS

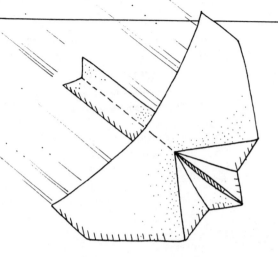

When people long ago wanted to fly, they looked to the birds for ideas. Birds made flying look easy. They just flapped their wings and away they went. Many people tried to imitate the birds: they built a pair of wings and flapped hard. They got a lot of exercise, but none of them actually managed to fly. They didn't realize that human muscles aren't strong enough to flap a person into the air.

But some people noticed that birds didn't always flap; sometimes they just extended their wings and glided. Maybe humans could glide, they thought, and they began experimenting.

Early gliding flights often ended in crashes. There was no way to control the glider's flight. Then, about a hundred years ago, a German named Otto Lilienthal learned to control gliders by hanging underneath them and shifting his body weight back and forth. The pilot's dangling legs also doubled as landing gear.

As more and more knowledge was gained, experimenters like the Wright brothers developed controls that were built in to gliders and eventually powered airplanes. Thanks to these and other pioneering efforts, we can now fly with the birds—although a bit more noisily.

The gliders you'll make in this section are all "fixed wing" gliders. Like birds gliding with their wings extended, these gliders have fixed, not flapping, wings. They also have controls to help them fly—and do some pretty amazing aerobatic maneuvers.

The Delta Dart

The Delta Dart starts out as a traditional paper airplane and then gets spiced up with flying controls that are the same as the controls on a full-sized plane. The name "Delta" comes from the triangle-shaped letter D in the Greek alphabet. You can see that the wing shape is a triangle. Delta wings rarely if ever occur in nature. It is a wing shape that was developed by humans. The Concorde supersonic airliner is an example of a full-sized airplane with a delta wing.

You'll need:
- a sheet of foolscap or writing paper slightly longer than it is wide
- sticky tape
- scissors
- ruler

1 Fold the paper in half the long way, then open it.

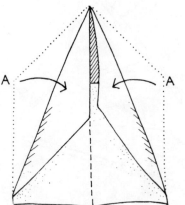

2 Fold the two corners in to the centre fold line.

CENTRE FOLD LINE.

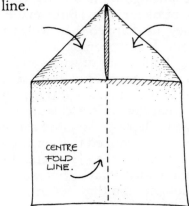

3 Fold corners A in to the centre fold line.

A   A

4 Fold over and crease.

5 Fold one side over to meet the centre fold line. Do the same with the other side.

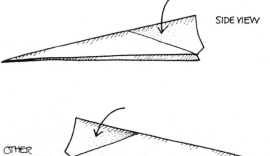

SIDE VIEW

OTHER SIDE VIEW

6 Swing the wings up into a horizontal position. The dart should come to a sharp point in front. If it doesn't, start again.

7 Tape the sides together as shown.

TAPE

If you try to fly your Delta Dart now, it will probably just dive into the ground. Turn the page to find out how to make it fly the way you want.

Feathered flyers

Next time you eat chicken, take a close look at the leftover bones. Like all birds, chickens have hollow bones with thin walls. They also have a delicate skeleton. Lightweight bones make it possible for birds to fly.

Bird feathers are light and airtight, providing a warm and aerodynamic covering. Feathers also give the wing the proper shape to fly. A bird without feathers can't fly because its wing is the wrong shape.

When people first tried to fly, they imitated the birds. They failed because strong, lightweight building materials hadn't yet been invented. Today we have aluminum and carbon fibre rods and other materials to help us fly (almost) like the birds.

Trimming the Delta Dart

The elevators

Many of the Delta gliders in this book will be nose heavy unless you give them flying controls to bring the nose up. The control that moves the nose of an airplane up or down is called the elevator. Here's how to make elevators for your Delta flyer.

1 Make four cuts in the tail as shown. Each should be about 1 cm (½ inch) long. The paper flaps between the cuts are the elevators.

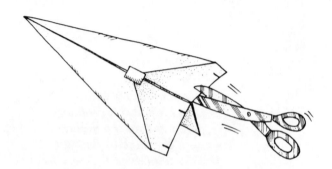

2 Bend the elevators up. The farther up the elevators are bent, the harder they will try to pull the nose up. So bend the elevators up only a little at first.

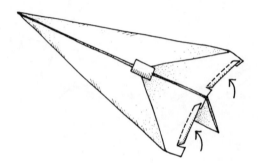

3 Test fly the Delta flyer to find the correct up angle for the elevators. If the Delta flyer still nose dives, bend the elevators up more. If it swoops and falls, reduce the up angle slightly.

The rudder

The control that moves the plane right or left is the rudder. Here's how to make a rudder for your Delta flyer.

1 Make a cut about 1 cm (½ inch) long on the vertical fin at the back of your glider.

2 To make the glider turn to the left, bend the rudder a bit to the left.

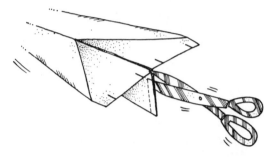

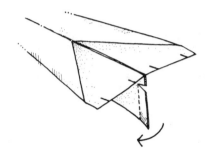

3 To make the glider turn to the right, bend the rudder to the right. The more the rudder is bent, the sharper the glider will turn. Also, the more the rudder is bent, the more steeply the glider dives. For tight turns it may be necessary to bend up the elevators to keep the glider from diving too steeply. Full-sized airplanes behave the same way; in a turn, the pilot has to pull up the nose to keep the plane from diving.

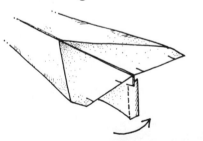

All airplanes need flying controls. These controls, operated by the pilot, overcome nose or tail heaviness and also enable the pilot to steer in any direction.

The ailerons

The controls that make the glider roll over one way or the other are called the ailerons. Because your Delta glider stays level when it flies, you don't need ailerons. However, if you want to do a roll, you can make the elevators behave like ailerons. Here's how.

1 Bend one elevator up and the other down.

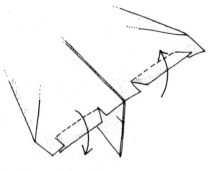

2 Give your glider a hard throw. The glider will roll in the direction of the elevator that is up.

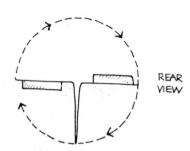

REAR VIEW

Elevators acting like ailerons occur on some full-sized airplanes too, for example, the Concorde. This combination of elevators and ailerons is called elevons!

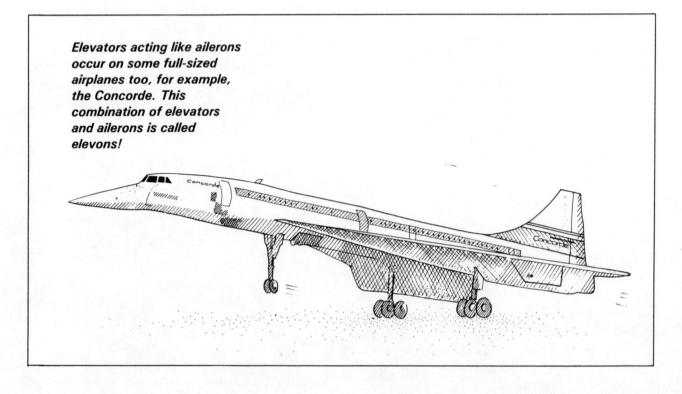

How controls change flight direction

Elevators, rudders and ailerons change how an airplane flies by changing the flow of air over the control. Let's take a closer look at how an elevators works.

If the elevator is flat, the airflow on both sides is equal and no change of direction takes place.

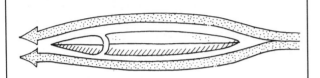

If the elevator is bent up, the airflow on the top slows down a little and the airflow on the bottom speeds up a little. This changes the pressure on the control so that now there is more pressure on the top. The airflow also pushes directly on the raised elevator causing even more downward pressure.

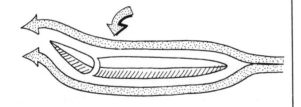

With more pressure on top, the elevator pulls the back part of the glider's wing down. As a result, the nose goes up.

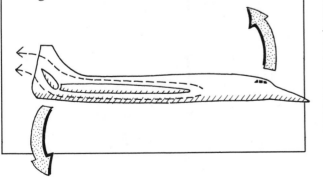

How it works

Here's an experiment to show that a difference in pressure does exist when there's more flow over one side of an object than over the other.

Hold a spoon lightly by the handle so that the bowl of the spoon slowly comes into contact with a stream of tap water. You might expect the water flow to push the spoon away but it doesn't. It sucks the spoon into the water flow. Why? There is flow where the water runs over the spoon and no flow where the air is sitting still on the other side of the spoon. Where there is more flow (on the water side) the pressure is lower, so the higher pressure on the air side forces the spoon into the stream of water.

This difference in pressure was discovered by Daniel Bernoulli about two hundred years ago. Today, understanding Bernoulli's principle is one of the requirements for getting a pilot's licence in North America.

The Delta Arrow

The Delta Arrow is a long-range Delta glider. With its large wing, it should cruise farther than the Delta Dart.

You'll need:
- a sheet of foolscap or writing paper slightly longer than it is wide
- scissors
- pencil
- ruler

1–4 Proceed as you did for the Delta Dart on page 10, but stop after step 4. Your glider should look like this:

5 Divide the end of each wing into three equal parts with a pencil. You will be folding your wing down on a line from the inner pencil mark to the nose tip.

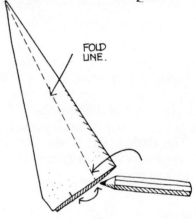

FOLD LINE.

6 Fold one wing down along the fold line.

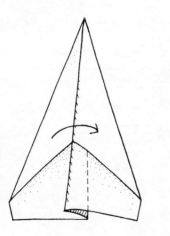

END VIEW

7 Do the same with the other wing. The wings should extend below the centre fold.

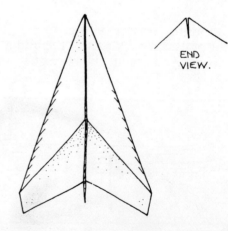

END VIEW.

8 Lift the wings into a horizontal position and tape as shown. Before flying the Delta Arrow, follow the trimming instructions on pages 12–14.

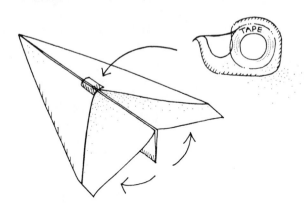

follow the trimming instructions on pages 12–14.

The big wing of the Delta Arrow lets it fly farther and slower than the Delta Dart. Do some test flights to find out other differences.

THE DELTA ARROW.

THE DELTA DART.

The four forces of flight

There are four forces acting on a paper airplane (or anything else that's flying).

If lift is greater than weight, the airplane goes up. If drag is greater than thrust, the airplane slows down. But if lift equals weight and thrust equals drag, the airplane will fly at a steady height and speed because the forces are all in balance.

LIFT.

THRUST

DRAG

WEIGHT

The Starship Delta

This Delta glider has turned-up wing tips, called winglets. These are also used on some real airplanes.

You'll need:
- a sheet of foolscap or writing paper slightly longer than it is wide
- pencil
- sticky tape
- scissors
- ruler

1–4 Proceed as you did for the Delta Dart but stop after step 4. Your glider should look like this:

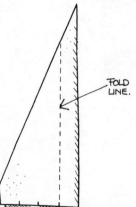

5 Divide the end of each wing into four equal parts with a pencil.

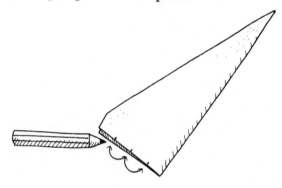

6 On one wing, make a fold as shown. Check that the fold goes from the pencil mark nearest the centre fold, parallel to the centre fold. Do not end the fold in the nose tip.

FOLD LINE.

7 Fold the wing down along the fold line.

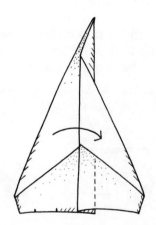

8 Do the same with the other wing.

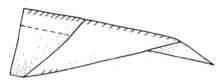

9 The side view should look like this. Fold the tips of each wing back. On most gliders this fold should start about 2 cm (¾ inch) from the wing tip. These are your winglets.

10 Swing the wings up and the winglets out as shown. Before flying the Starship Delta, follow the trimming instructions on pages 12–14.

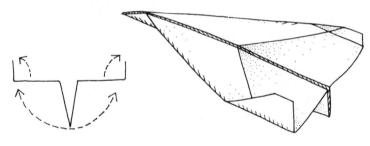

Outdoor flying

All of the Delta gliders fly well outdoors. If the wind blows your glider around too much, add some weight by attaching one or two paperclips to the bottom, about halfway between the nose and tail.

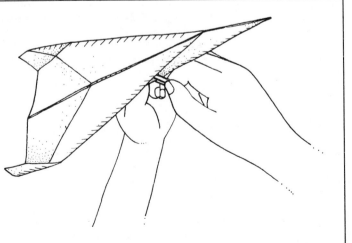

The Origami Aerobat

This is one of the world's best paper airplane designs. The type of paper folding used to make it was invented in Japan and is called origami. To make a good flyer, follow the folding instructions carefully. Try not to fold or wrinkle the paper where it isn't supposed to be folded.

You'll need:
- a sheet of foolscap or writing paper 18 cm × 28 cm (7½ × 11 inches)
- scissors
- pencil
- ruler

1 Cut a strip of paper 5 cm (2 inches) wide from the top of the paper. This will be your Aerobat's tail.

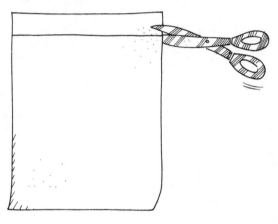

2 Make a crease down the centre of the tail and fold the ends up as shown. Set the tail aside.

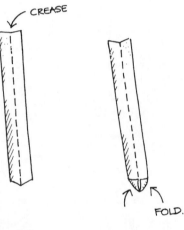

3 Mark B for bottom and T for top on either side of your piece of paper.

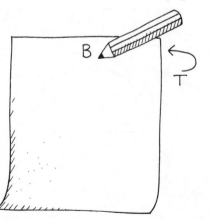

4 With B up, fold one edge over to meet the other side, then open so that you can see a crease. Do the same with the other edge.

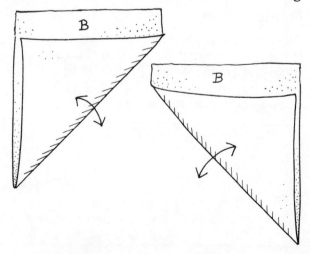

5 When you open the paper, it should have creases that look like this:

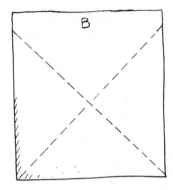

6 Turn the paper over so that T is up and fold as shown. Unfold to leave a crease.

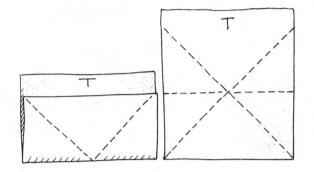

7 Turn the paper over again so that B is up. Bend in the two sides as shown and press flat.

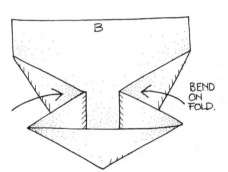

8 Fold as shown.

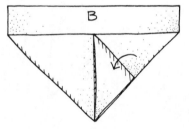

9 Fold and open up to leave a crease.

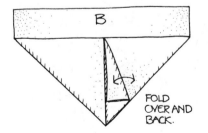

10 Fold and open up to leave a crease.

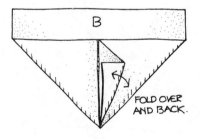

11 You should now have creases that cross like this:

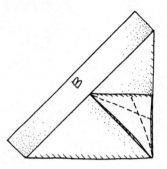

12 Fold in the crease lines and pinch up the centre as shown.

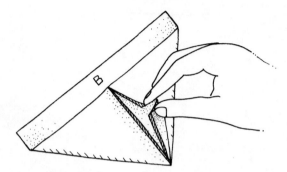

13 Fold the pinched-up portion towards the nose.

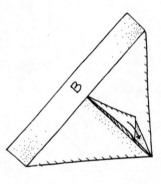

14 Repeat steps 8 to 13 on the other side. Your Aerobat should look like this when you're done:

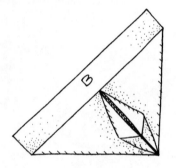

15 Fold the nose point under along the line indicated by the dots.

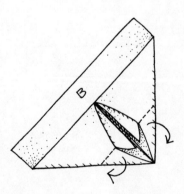

16 Pull the split nose up. Your Aerobat should look like this:

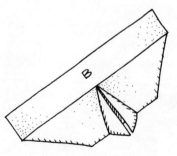

17
Fold the plane in half to make a crease.

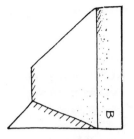

18
Unfold the plane and pull the rest of the nose up again.

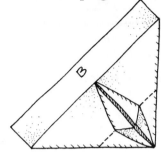

19
Insert the tail as shown.

TURN OVER.

20
Refold the nose down, leaving the split nose up.

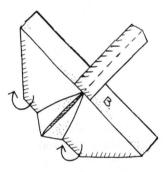

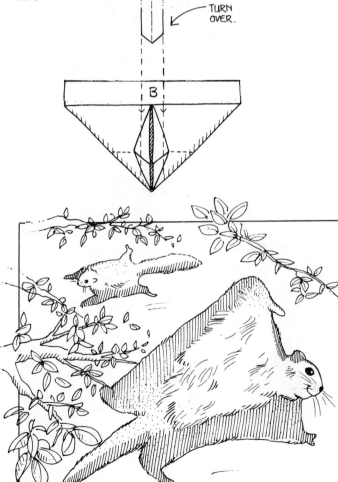

Furry flyers

North American flying squirrels don't really fly—they glide, just like your paper airplanes. A flying squirrel has a flattened body shape and loose skin between its front and back legs. By stretching out its legs, it pulls the loose skin tight. The tight skin acts as a wing, allowing it to glide from tree to tree. As it glides, the squirrel's "wing" curves up slightly in a natural dihedral angle.

A flying squirrel uses its tail to steer. Seen from above, a flying squirrel looks a lot like the Origami Aerobat, which also uses a tail to keep it straight.

Trimming the Origami Aerobat

Your Origami Aerobat will probably need a few adjustments before it will fly properly. Here's how to trim your Aerobat.

1 Turn the Aerobat over so that T is up.

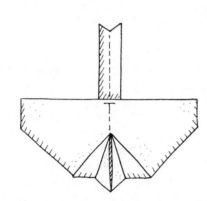

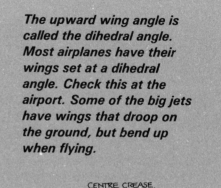

The upward wing angle is called the dihedral angle. Most airplanes have their wings set at a dihedral angle. Check this at the airport. Some of the big jets have wings that droop on the ground, but bend up when flying.

2 Fold the Aerobat along the centre crease so that the wings are bent up slightly.

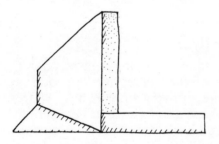

3 Throw the Aerobat gently. It should glide almost straight ahead or turn gently to one side. If it does, you're in luck; you don't need to make any further adjustments.

4 If the Aerobat does tight turns or spins down, make sure it isn't wrinkled or bent out of shape, then increase the dihedral angle (bend the wings up more).

5 If adjusting the dihedral angle doesn't work, make a gull wing fold. To do this, fold up on the centre crease and out on the outer fold lines.

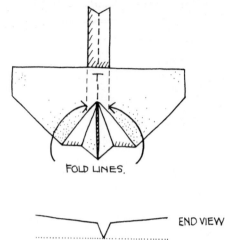

FOLD LINES.

END VIEW

6 If your Aerobat still doesn't fly well, try bending down the wing tips.

TIPS BENT DOWN

7 If nothing works, put the Aerobat aside. No two paper airplanes fly the same. Don't feel badly if yours doesn't fly well—just make another.

Aerobat Aerobatics

Fly the Aerobat by holding it between the thumb and forefinger and throwing it gently. Once you've got the hang of flying it, try these aerobatics.

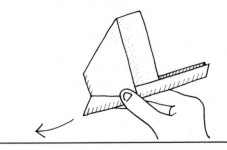

The steady glide
Throw gently, letting the Aerobat ease out of your hand.

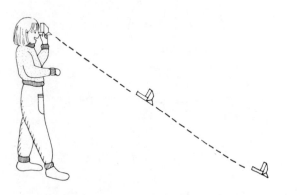

The swoop
Throw straight ahead, medium hard.

The loop
Throw HARD!

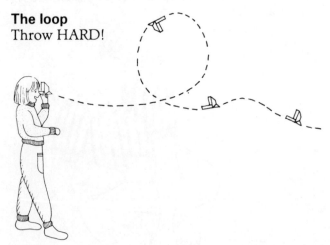

The half loop
Hold the Aerobat as shown upside down over your head. Hold it to one side so that it won't hit your body when it falls. Drop it.

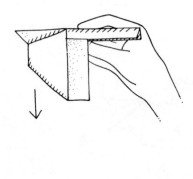

The nosedive

Hold the Aerobat by the tail high in the air. The nose should point straight down. When you drop it, it will do a steep dive and should straighten out just before it hits the ground. If it doesn't work, try standing on a chair to give yourself more height.

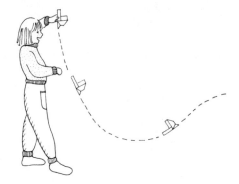

The tail slide

Hold the Aerobat nose up. The tail should point straight down. Drop it. The Aerobat should snap around from tail down to nose down and dive away. If it doesn't, try standing on a chair to give yourself more height.

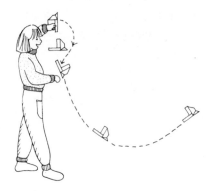

The tail toss

Hold the Aerobat as shown and throw it tail first as if it were a ball. The aerobat will flip around as it leaves your hand and may do some exciting aerobatics. The tail toss takes some practice but it's worth it; it results in higher, longer flights.

The flick roll

Hold the Aerobat by one wing and throw it as you would a Frisbee. You might be surprised at what happens.

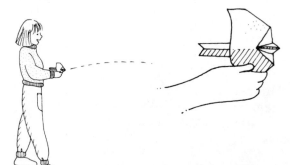

A properly made Origami Aerobat is a stable airplane — that is, it always wants to glide upright and straight no matter how it's thrown. The way you build it and bend the wings insures that it will be stable. Airplane designers strive to make real airplanes stable too, because stable airplanes are safer and easier to fly.

Aerobat Test Pilot Experiments

Once you have some flying experience with the Origami Aerobat, try some test pilot flights.

Flat flyer

What happens when you flatten the Aerobat, removing the dihedral angle completely?

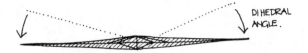

DIHEDRAL ANGLE.

Pug-nose landing gear

Push back the nose of the Aerobat so that the bottom opens out as shown. You now have landing gear. This pug-nose design also changes the Aerobat's flying speed. Try it and see.

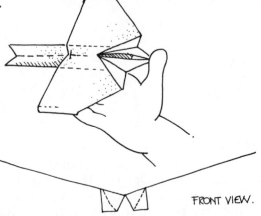

FRONT VIEW.

Tail redesign

Try removing the tail. What happens when you fly it? Now put the tail back in and see how it flies.

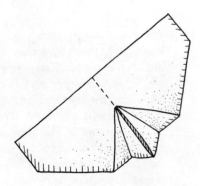

Straight as an arrow

It's not the weight of the tail that keeps the Aerobat flying straight but the flow of air *against* the tail. The tail of an airplane keeps the airplane straight just like the feathers keep an arrow straight as it sails through the air.

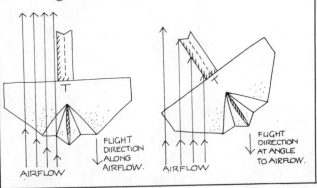

FLIGHT DIRECTION ALONG AIRFLOW.

AIRFLOW

FLIGHT DIRECTION AT ANGLE TO AIRFLOW.

AIRFLOW

Add some weight

1 Attach a paperclip to the nose of your Aerobat and fly it.

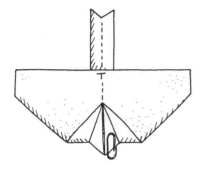

2 Next attach the paperclip to the tail. Fly it again.

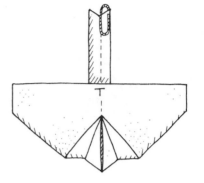

3 If your Aerobat nosedives with the clip on its nose and flutters or flops end over end with the clip on its tail, you're not alone. The paperclip upsets the aerodynamic balance of the plane and changes the way it flies.

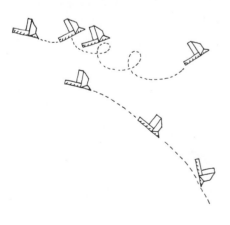

Weight and balance are important in full-sized planes too. When an airplane is loaded, it can carry only a certain amount of weight, and the weight must be loaded so the plane's balance isn't upset by having too much weight in the nose or tail.

The Origami Twin Tail

This speedy twin-tailed origami airplane is based on the Origami Aerobat.

You'll need:
- a sheet of foolscap or writing paper 18 cm × 28 cm (7½2 × 11 inches)
- scissors
- pencil
- ruler

1–16 Follow steps 3 to 16 for the Origami Aerobat on pages 20–22. Your glider should look like this:

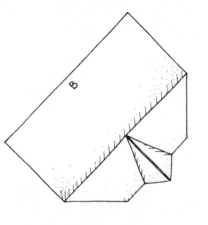

17 Turn the glider over so that T is up and bend the wings up together.

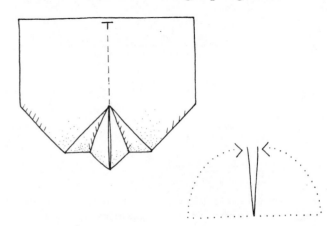

18 Hold the wings together and make two cuts as shown.

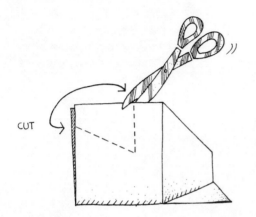

CUT

19 Fold the edges of the tail up along the fold lines as shown. These are your plane's rudders.

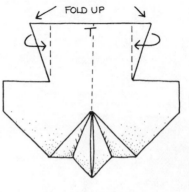

FOLD UP

RUDDERS FORMED BY FOLDED UP TAIL

Trimming the Twin Tail

1 Trim the Origami Twin Tail by adjusting the dihedral angle of the wings. For help on how to do this, see page 24.

2 Make sure the rudders are always straight up and down, not bent at an angle. Fly the Twin Tail the same as you did the Origami Aerobat (see page 26).

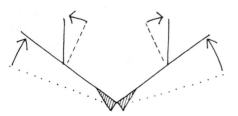

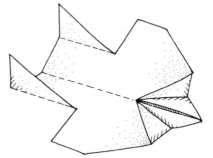

The gull wing twin tail

1 Make two fold lines as shown.

2 Fold the wings up as shown.

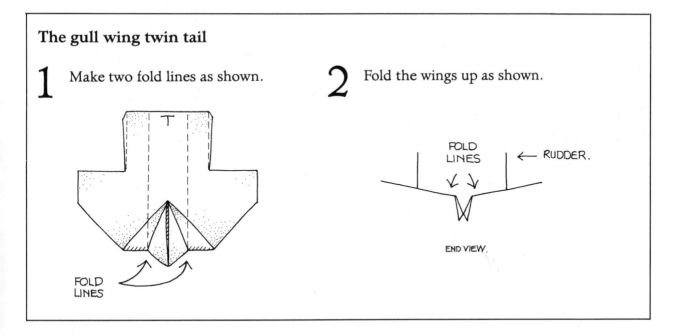

FOLD LINES

FOLD LINES

FOLD LINES

← RUDDER.

END VIEW.

The Flying Meat Tray (FMT)

Save the Styrofoam from under meat or vegetables and try this super flyer.

You'll need:
- a clean Styrofoam meat tray
- a felt pen or marker
- sticky tape
- scissors
- ruler

1 Trim off the curved edges of the meat tray and cut the flat piece that remains into a square.

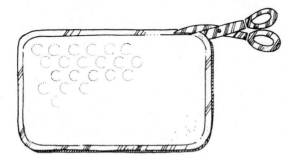

2 With a marker, draw a triangle on the Styrofoam. Cut along the lines with scissors. You will use the big triangle as the FMT's wings and one of the small triangles as the fins and rudder. Throw away the other small triangle.

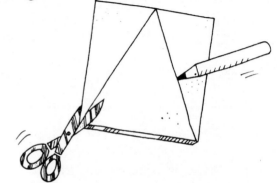

3 Cut a slot to the midpoint of the large triangle. The slot should be just wide enough so that another piece of Styrofoam will fit into it snuggly.

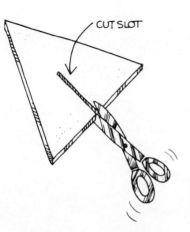

CUT SLOT

4 Cut a slot not quite to the midpoint of the rudder as shown. This slot should be the same width as the other one.

CUT SLOT

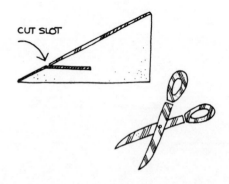

5 Cut the front of the rudder off at an angle as shown.

6 Push the rudder into the wing so that the two slots fit together.

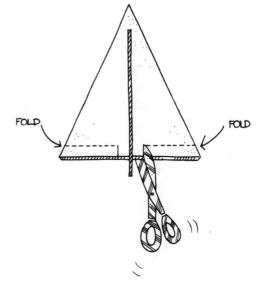

7 If the rudder is loose, tape it to the wing. When fitted in, the rudder should stick out a little past the end of the wing. Make a fold line on the rudder as shown.

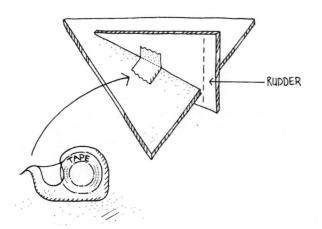

RUDDER

8 Make a 1 cm (½ inch) long cut on each side of the rudder. Then make a fold line as shown. These flaps are your elevators.

FOLD   FOLD

Trimming the FMT

When you first make it, the FMT is out of balance. Here's how to get it flying properly.

---

1 Use paperclips for the nose weight. For a small FMT, one or two paperclips will be enough. For a larger FMT, you may need more paperclips or even have to tape on a coin.

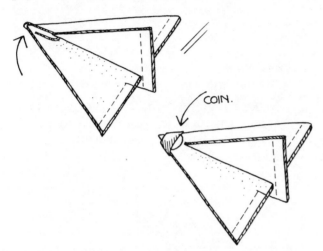

COIN.

2 Straighten the rudder and bend the elevators up slightly.

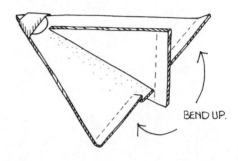

BEND UP.

3 Throw your FMT in a gentle glide. If it dives to the ground, try more up elevator or less nose weight.

4 If the FMT glides slowly and falls in a series of swoops, try less up elevator or add more nose weight. Keep adjusting the elevators and nose weight until you're satisfied with the glide.

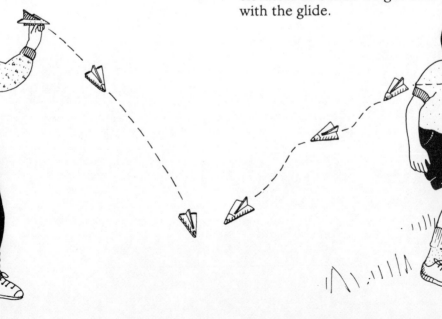

5 To make the FMT turn, bend the rudder slightly. Make sure both elevators are bent equally.

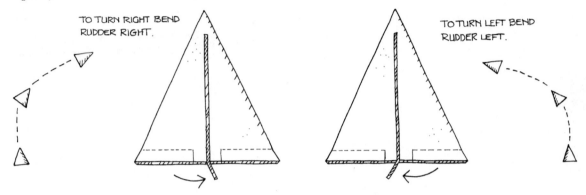

TO TURN RIGHT BEND RUDDER RIGHT.

TO TURN LEFT BEND RUDDER LEFT.

Flying fish!!!

Flying fish are small and (poor them) tasty. To avoid being eaten by hungry predators, they have developed long front fins that act like wings when the fish jumps out of the water. To get airborne, the flying fish swims fast and then shoots out of the water, gliding for some distance before falling back in. Flying fish can't control their ''flights''; their fish tails don't steer very well. But even so, their flights are impressive for a fish. As Samuel Johnson once said, ''Like a dog walking on its hind legs it is not done well; but you are surprised to find it done at all.''

FMT Aerobatics

Once your FMT is flying well, try these aerobatic maneuvers.

The loop
Throw the FMT straight ahead HARD.

The high speed turn
Throw the FMT hard with one wing down.

Fooling around with the FMT

What happens when you change the wing and tail shape of the FMT? Does it fly better or worse? Try the shapes below, then experiment with your own designs. If you make several different wing and body shapes, you can try various combinations.

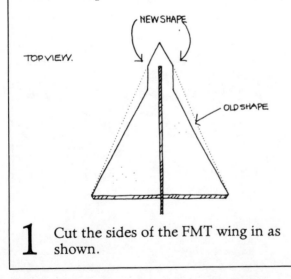

1 Cut the sides of the FMT wing in as shown.

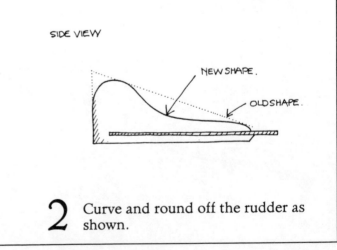

2 Curve and round off the rudder as shown.

Is it a bird? Is it a plane?

Birds have developed different wing shapes for different kinds of flight. These same shapes are used by aircraft designers for special kinds of flight.

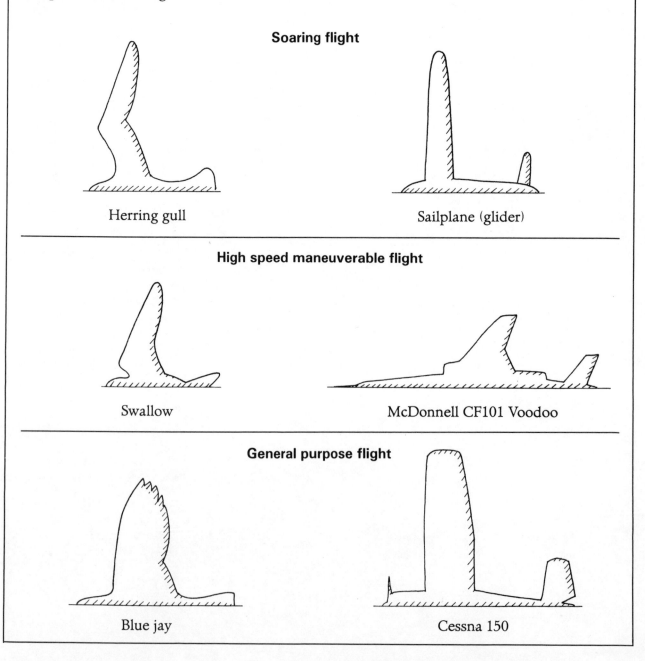

Soaring flight

Herring gull

Sailplane (glider)

High speed maneuverable flight

Swallow

McDonnell CF101 Voodoo

General purpose flight

Blue jay

Cessna 150

TWIRLING WINGS

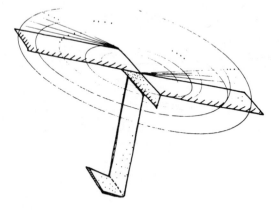

The idea of a twirling or turning wing, rather than a fixed wing, has been around for a long time. Nature thought of it first. Watch a maple tree seed spinning down from a tree and you will see that it gets where it's going by twirling through the air.

When people tried to use turning wings to fly, there were problems. For one thing, spinning seeds don't get dizzy but people do. In a spinning aircraft, a pilot would rotate along with the wings and would twirl to the ground dizzy or sick or both. When attempts were made to have the pilot sit on a platform and use his muscle power to turn the wings, the platform would rotate in the opposite direction to the wings.

However the advantage to using turning wings to take off straight up was so great that the experimenters persisted. They first succeeded in producing an autogiro, which was a bit like an airplane and helicopter combined. It had both an overhead turning wing and an engine and propeller, but it had to move forward to take off. Finally a true helicopter was invented that could take off straight up.

Twirling wing flyers are easy to make and terrific flyers. Once you've made the ones in this section, try experimenting with some designs of your own.

The Dirigible

This is probably the easiest flying machine to make in the whole book. It does a steep glide, rotating furiously as it falls.

You'll need:
- a sheet of foolscap or writing paper
- scissors

1 Cut a piece of paper into a strip about 2 cm x 21 cm (¾ x 8¼ inches).

2 Make a cut at each end of the paper strip as shown. Be sure that each cut goes only halfway across the paper, and that the cuts are on opposite sides.

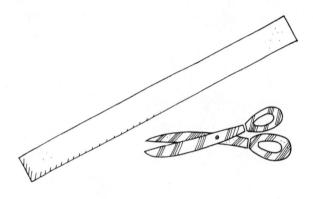

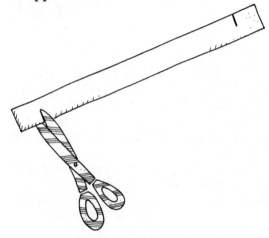

3 Bend the paper (do not fold it) so that the two cuts fit into each other.

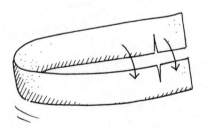

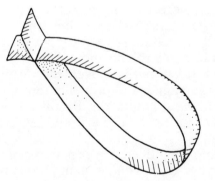

Flying the Dirigible

Flying the Dirigible is a snap. Just hold it above your head and drop it. As it falls, it will start spinning and look like a dirigible. The spinning makes it stable in the air. Try flying your Dirigible from some place high—from the top of some stairs, for instance.

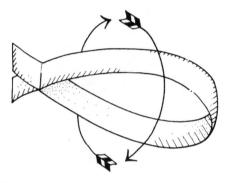

How big a dirigible can you make and fly? How small?

Floaters

A real-life dirigible has a rigid framework that is covered in cloth. Gas bags inside the framework make it float in the air. A blimp, on the other hand, is just a big cigar-shaped bag filled with gas and pressurized air. It doesn't have a rigid framework.

Both dirigibles and blimps are moved through the air by engines and propellers that are controlled by a pilot seated in a cabin called a control gondola.

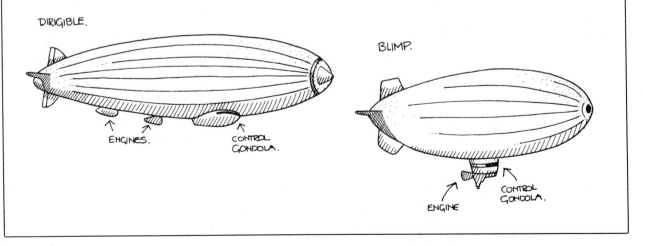

The Rotoglide

Round and round and down . . . the Rotoglide will sail with its wings twirling around like a helicopter rotor blade.

You'll need:
- a sheet of foolscap or writing paper
- scissors
- a pencil

1 Cut out a piece of paper as shown. Cut out along the solid lines and draw on the dotted lines with a pencil.

2 Fold A and B in opposite directions.

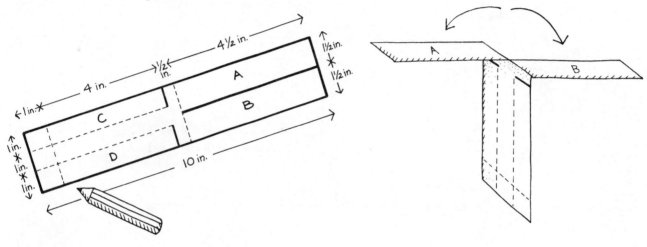

3 Fold C and D towards each other so that they overlap.

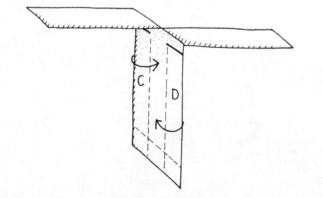

4 Fold the bottom up.

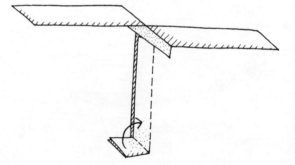

Flying the Rotoglide

1 Hold the Rotoglide over your head and drop it. It will glide to the floor spinning. The higher you start your Rotoglide's flight, the farther it will go.

2 If your Rotoglide wobbles, add a paperclip or other small weight to the bottom.

One-wing Rotoglides

Next time you see a maple key spinning down, think of your Rotoglide. Even though a maple key (seed) has only one "wing," the rotary (gyroscopic) action keeps it stable. By gliding in this way, seeds get away from the parent plant, so they have a better chance to grow.

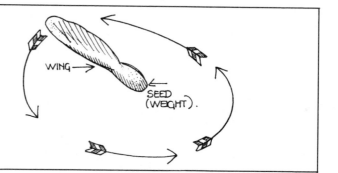

Helicopters can glide down with their rotors twirling even if the engine fails.

The Heliostraw

This rotary glider not only glides—it can also climb and hover.

You'll need:
- cardboard (the kind from the back of a pad of paper works well)
- a plastic drinking straw
- masking tape
- scissors
- ruler

1 Cut a piece of cardboard 2 cm x 21 cm (¾ x 8¼ inches). Draw two lines from corner to corner to find the centre point.

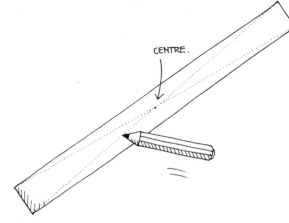

CENTRE.

2 Make a hole at the centre point that is slightly bigger than the width (diameter) of the straw. Use a hole punch or the point of a pair of scissors to make this hole.

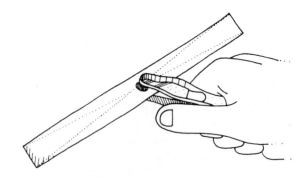

3 Make cuts 1 cm (½ inch) long on either side of the hole as shown. This is your Heliostraw's wing.

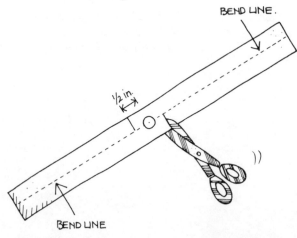

BEND LINE.

½ in.

BEND LINE

4 Wrap tape around one end of the straw so that the wrapped end is a snug fit when put into the hole in the wing. If the wing wobbles, tape the straw to the wing to hold it firm.

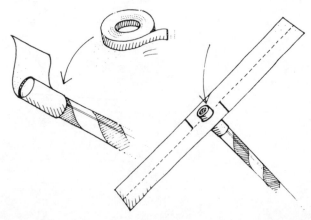

5 Fold under the last 1 cm (½ inch) of the wing tips. Tape these folds down. This will add weight to the wing tips and increase momentum as the wings spin.

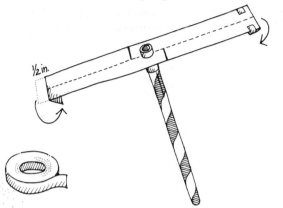

6 From the cuts outward, bend the wings down slightly along the fold line. Do not bend the wings down too far. There should be just a gentle curve. Make sure both wings are bent down the same amount.

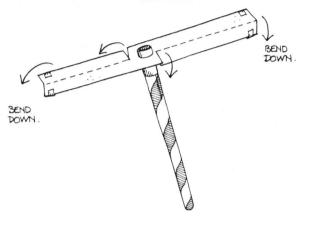

How it works

To get lift, there has to be movement of air over a wing. The Delta and Origami gliders you made earlier in the book get air movement over the wing by gliding through the air. Rotary wing gliders like the Rotoglide get air movement by twirling their wings through the air.

On windy days small planes on the ground can get so much air flowing over their wings that they get lifted off the ground and flipped upside down. That's why small planes are usually tied down.

Trimming and Flying the Heliostraw

1 To fly the Heliostraw, hold the straw between your palms. Roll your palms together so that the wing rotates rapidly counterclockwise. Let go. The Heliostraw will spin out of your hand.

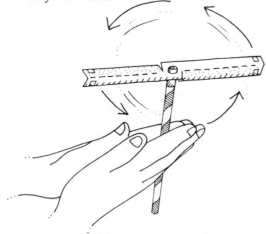

2 If the wing spins but the Heliostraw won't climb, bend the edge of the wings down more. If the Heliostraw climbs rapidly but stops spinning almost immediately, try reducing the amount of bend at the wing edge. Experiment to find the wing setting that works best for you.

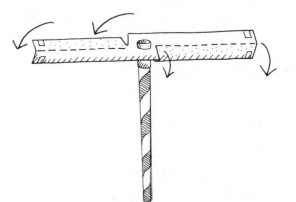

Helio-copter

Your Heliostraw flies just like a helicopter. When the helicopter's rotor is tilted, it flies in the direction of the tilt.

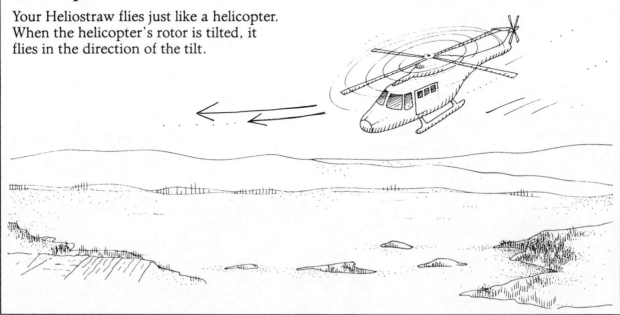

Heliostraw Aerobatics

Once you've mastered flying your Heliostraw, try these mid-air maneuvers.

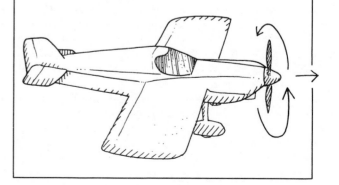

Try different sizes and shapes of wings. Or even four wings instead of two.

The glide

Spin the Heliostraw gently backwards (clockwise) and let it go. It will spin down just like the Rotoglide.

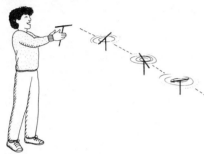

The hover

Hold the straw straight up and down and fly the Heliostraw. It should climb and hover before gliding down.

Fast forward

Tilt the straw away from you and fly it.

Propellers

Turn the rotating wings of the Heliostraw sideways and you have a propeller. If you try to fly the Heliostraw when it is tilted like this, it will just fly into the ground. A propeller must be attached to something that has lift (such as the wings of an airplane) or it won't work properly. The wings provide the lift and the propeller provides the forward motion.

47

WHAT IS IT?

In the world of flying and airplanes, there are always a few what-is-its around. What-is-its are airplanes that don't look like anything else that is flying at the time. Some have round, saucer-shaped wings, others have as many as 30 small wings, while still others have circular wings or no wings at all.

These what-is-its can fly, but not usually as well as more ordinary looking airplanes. Even so, information about how what-is-its fly can be very useful in designing other airplanes. For example, knowledge gained by flying wingless what-is-its (called "lifting bodies" because the body shape, rather than the wing, provides lift) was used in designing the Space Shuttle.

As long as people have the desire to experiment, what-is-its will continue to be made and flown. Have fun experimenting with the unusual what-is-its in this section.

The Straw Glider

The straw glider has round, or "circular," wings. Circular wings have been tried on full-sized airplanes almost since the beginning of aviation, but they have never been very successful. On the Straw Glider they work very well.

You'll need:
- a sheet of foolscap or writing paper
- a plastic drinking straw
- sticky tape
- scissors
- ruler

1 Cut the drinking straw so that it is 21 cm (8¼ inches) long.

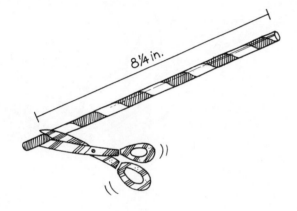

2 Cut two strips of paper, one 2 cm x 16 cm (¾ × 6¼ inches) and the other 1.5 cm x 14 cm (½ × 5½ inches).

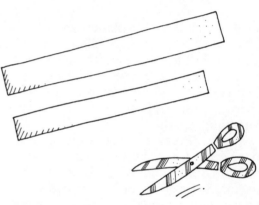

3 Bend the large strip of paper into a circle so that the ends overlap slightly and tape as shown. The overlap will form a pocket into which the straw will fit.

4 Pry open the pocket and slip it over one end of the straw.

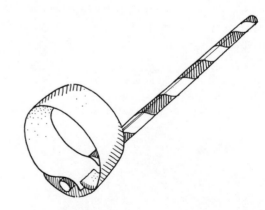

5 Bend the smaller strip of paper into a circle and tape it the same way you did before. Slip it over the other end of the straw.

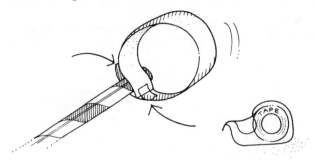

6 Move the two paper circles (the circular wings) until they are both positioned above the straw as shown. Tape them in place.

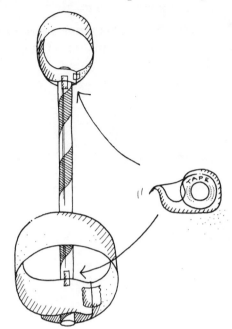

7 Looking down on the glider, make sure that the wings are at right angles to the straw. If they're not, loosen the tape and re-tape them so they are straight.

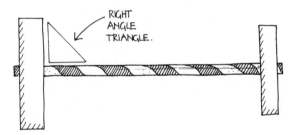

RIGHT ANGLE TRIANGLE.

It sure doesn't look like it'll fly. But wait till you give it a try.

Trimming and Flying the Straw Glider

1 To fly the Straw Glider, hold it by the straw with the smaller wing to the front and throw gently.

2 If the glider nose dives, move the large wing forward slightly and try again. If you move it too far forward, the glider will wobble through the air.

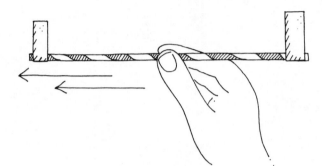

3 If the glider wobbles when you first fly it, move the small wing back slightly and try again. Properly adjusted, the glider should have a long, flat glide.

What happens when you try to fly the Straw Glider backwards, with the large wing in front?

No turns

When your Straw Glider is properly trimmed, it will always fly in a straight line. Even if it is tilted when you throw it, the straw will swing down as soon as it leaves your hand so that the glide is straight.

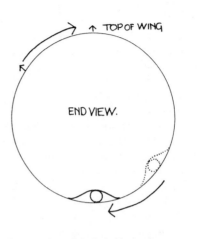

Glider thrown with wings tilted.

Straw (weight) falls to bottom.

How it works

The top and bottom of the wings provide the lift, and the sides of the wings act like the tail on the Origami Aerobat and keep the plane flying straight.

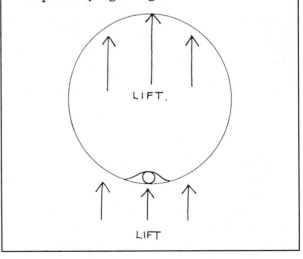

The Twirl-o-Tube

Lightweight tubes can fly, if a few changes are made to them. The secret is to add weight to the front and make the tube spin, or rotate, while in the air. The Twirl-o-Tube won't win any prizes as a flyer, but it's fun to fly once you get the hang of it.

You'll need:
- the cardboard tube from a roll of paper towels or toilet paper
- heavy tape such as masking tape
- scissors
- ruler

1 Measure the distance across the end of the tube. This is called the diameter. Cut the tube so that it is the same length or just a bit longer than the diameter. This tube had a diameter of 4 cm (1½ inches), so it was cut 4 cm (1½ inches) long.

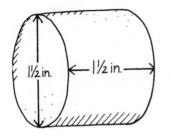

2 Wrap a layer of heavy tape around one end as shown.

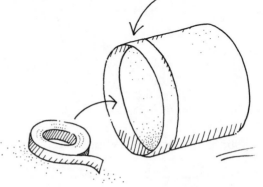

Trimming and Flying the Twirl-o-Tube

1 Throw the tube so that it goes tape end forward and rotates at the same time. To do this, try an underhand throw. Let the tube roll off your fingers as you throw to give it a spin. Even though the Twirl-o-Tube may not fly very well at first, you must perfect your throwing technique before you can trim the tube to make it fly better.

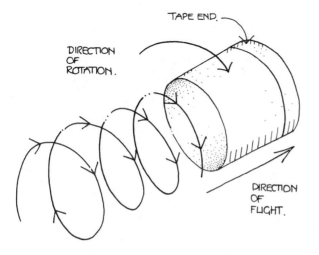

TAPE END.

DIRECTION OF ROTATION.

DIRECTION OF FLIGHT.

2 Once you've got the throwing technique down pat, you may notice some flying problems. If the tube wobbles as it flies, add another layer of tape to the nose and try again. Keep adding tape to the nose until the wobble is almost gone.

If the tube gets too heavy and will not glide far, take some of the tape off. You may not be able to eliminate the wobble completely because the paper tube may be a bit too heavy to begin with.

How it works

Twirl-o-Tubes are circular flying wings without bodies, or "fuselages." Airplane designers know that a flying wing makes a very efficient airplane; it doesn't have a fuselage to weigh it down. But no really successful full-sized flying wing has been built for two reasons. First, with no fuselage, there's nowhere to store cargo, baggage or even a crew. Secondly, there are problems with stability.

Your Twirl-o-Tube doesn't have stability problems because it spins as it flies. Spinning makes things stable. Just think of a spinning top. When a circular object is spinning and stable, it is called a gyroscope. The gyroscopic action of the spinning Twirl-o-Tube keeps it steady and stable in flight.

The Super Twirl-o-Tube

An aluminum can makes a terrific Twirl-o-Tube, but it's more difficult to make. Ask an adult to help you when cutting the can.

You'll need:
- an aluminum soft drink can
- heavy tape such as masking tape
- sticky tape
- scissors that won't be ruined by cutting aluminum
- ruler

1 Work a hole in the side of the can with the point of the scissors, then cut all the way around one end of the can. Be careful to avoid metal splinters when you cut the aluminum.

2 The cut end will have a few sharp points on it. Carefully cut off the sharp points. The can may also be bent. After you have removed the sharp bits, bend the can back into a circle.

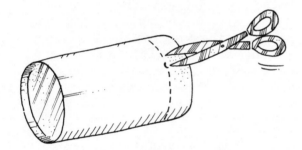

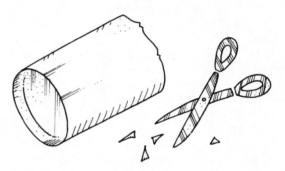

3 Measure the distance across the the end of the can (the diameter). Cut the other end of the can off so that the length is the same as the diameter. Again, be sure to remove any sharp pieces.

4 Put a single layer of heavy tape at one end of the tube as shown. This is the front of your Super Twirl-o-Tube. On the other end put a single layer of sticky tape. The end with the sticky tape is the back.

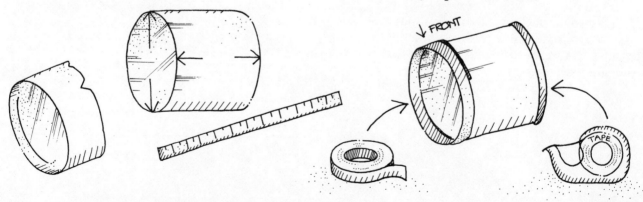

5 Follow the directions on page 55 for trimming and flying your Super Twirl-o-Tube.

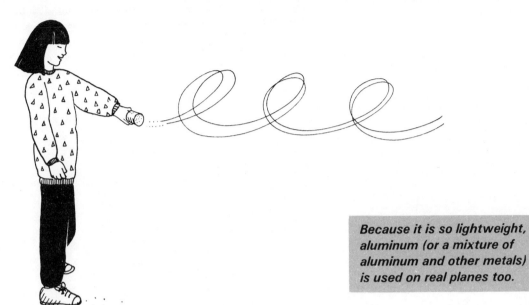

> Because it is so lightweight, aluminum (or a mixture of aluminum and other metals) is used on real planes too.

Other gyroflyers

Probably the best known gyroflyer is the Frisbee. It was invented by some bakery workers fooling around with pie plates during their lunch hour. They found what a lot of people had discovered before: that a flat round object will fly if you throw it with some spin on it. Today there are all kinds of Frisbees, but a good old-fashioned lightweight pie plate still works pretty well.

PARACHUTES

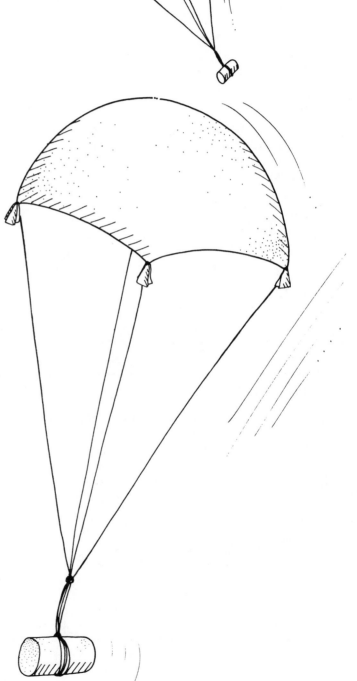

Parachutes were first thought of long ago. In fact, parachutes were probably the first practical flying device. But for a long time, no one bothered making one. Why not? Until balloons and planes were invented, there wasn't really any need for them.

When balloons began to be flown, people started jumping out of them. The earliest recorded parachute jumps from balloons were made around 1800. These jumps were just stunts, but people soon recognized the value of parachutes as life-saving devices.

Even though parachutes were developed long before World War I, Canadian and British airplane crews didn't use them in that war. They weren't allowed to. Their commanders believed that having parachutes on board an aircraft would be too much of a temptation for crews. After all, they might jump out if there was danger!

Today parachute jumping is still the standard way of escaping from a crashing airplane. Sport jumping is done just for fun.

The Tissue-Chute

This small, light parachute is great for indoor flying. It's too delicate for outdoors.

You'll need:
- Kleenex or other paper tissue
- sewing thread
- scissors
- measuring tape or ruler
- a small paperclip or other small object to use as a weight

1 Cut your tissue so that it's square. Most tissues have two layers. If possible, separate the layers and use only one to make the Tissue-Chute.

2 Cut four pieces of thread. Each piece should be twice as long as one side of the tissue. So if your tissue measures 19 cm (7½ inches) along one side, each string should be twice that long, or 38 cm (15 inches).

Parachute parts

On a full-sized parachute, the tissue paper part is called a canopy and the threads are called shroud lines. There are many more shroud lines on a full-sized chute.

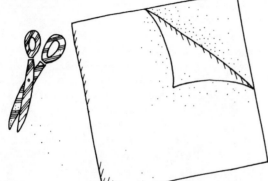

60

3 Tie one thread to each corner of the tissue.

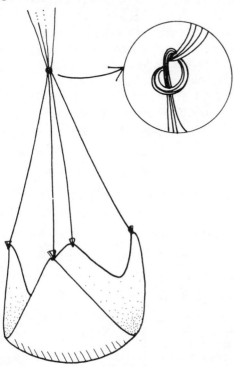

4 Hold all four threads together and let the tissue hang. Tie the four threads together in a knot about halfway between the tissue and the thread ends. Check that the threads are the same length from the knot to the tissue. If they aren't, try again. When they are the same length, tie another knot over the first one.

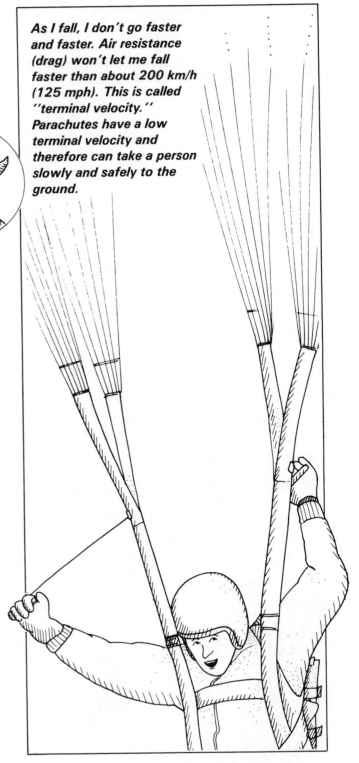

As I fall, I don't go faster and faster. Air resistance (drag) won't let me fall faster than about 200 km/h (125 mph). This is called "terminal velocity." Parachutes have a low terminal velocity and therefore can take a person slowly and safely to the ground.

Flying the Tissue-Chute

1 Tie a paperclip or other light weight to the thread below the knot.

2 Hold the Tissue-Chute high in the air by the top of the tissue. Check that the threads aren't tangled and let it drop.

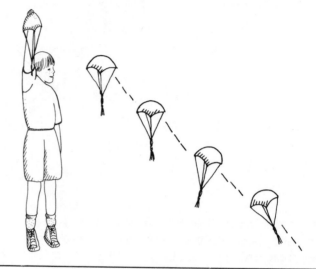

Nature's parachutists

This summer, watch a dandelion seed float through the air. It's a mini-parachute. Instead of a solid canopy, it and other seed parachutists have a canopy made of thin fibres. These fibres make such a good canopy and the seeds are so lightweight that they are often carried upwards by air currents.

The same thing has happened to human parachutists who are forced to jump in or near storms. Violent updrafts send them up instead of down. One pilot coming down by parachute was caught in storm updrafts for more than 15 minutes. During that time, he was tossed around and pelted with hailstones.

Many spiders use parachutes just minutes after they hatch. The newborn spider spins out a tangle of thin web material and dangles it until a puff of wind carries it (and the spider) away.

3 If it falls too fast, the weight is too heavy. Replace it with a lighter weight.

4 If it falls slowly but swings wildly from side to side, the weight is too light. Add a bit more weight. Keep experimenting until your Tissue-Chute drops slowly and swings gently.

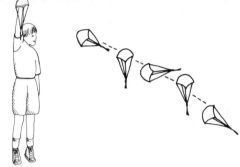

Parachutes then and now

The first practical parachute design was sketched more than 500 years ago by Leonardo da Vinci. Leonardo drew a parachute that had a solid framework at the bottom, was pyramid shaped and appeared to be supported by ribs, instead of being collapsible like a modern parachute. There is no evidence that it was ever tried out.

Many of today's sport parachutes are parafoils. These are a double thickness of rectangular cloth open at one end. Air whooshes in between the two layers of cloth, giving the parafoil a wing-like shape. This shape allows the parafoil to glide forward like an airplane wing. By pulling strings attached to the edges, the parafoil can be steered. Parafoils also make good kites.

Someone has even built a para*plane*. It has a seat, two engines and a propeller hanging from a parafoil that acts like a wing.

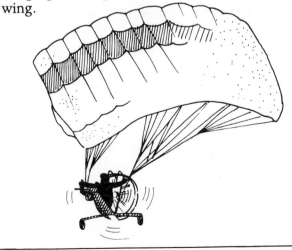

The Heavy Duty Chute

To make a parachute suitable for outdoors, you need something larger and stronger than the Tissue-Chute. The sky's the limit for long, high flights outdoors with this Heavy Duty Chute.

You'll need:

- a square cloth handkerchief or scarf
- light string
- scissors
- measuring tape or ruler
- a weight

1 Proceed as you did in steps 2-4 of the Tissue-Chute on pages 60–61.

Flying The Heavy Duty Chute

1 Tie a weight to the shroud lines below the knot.

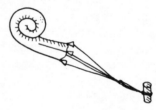

2 Hold the parachute by the centre of the canopy and roll it up towards the weight. Keep folding the sides in so that the roll of cloth is neat.

3 Finish by wrapping the shroud lines around the roll of cloth. The weight must be on the outside or the shroud lines will become tangled when the parachute is thrown.

4 Throw the parachute as high as possible into the air.

5 If the Heavy Duty Chute falls too fast, try a lighter weight. If it falls too slowly and swings from side to side, use a heavier weight. Even with an ideal weight, your parachute will always swing slightly. Real parachutes often have a hole in the top of the canopy to change the air flow and reduce the swinging.

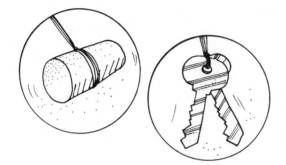

S-L-O-W down

Parachutes are sometimes used to help fast jet planes slow down after landing. The parachute is stored in a small container at the back of the jet and is popped out when the jet has landed and is travelling along the runway.

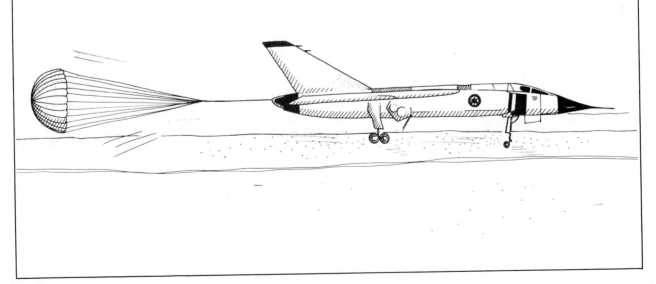

KITES

Kites have a long and interesting history. No one knows who flew the first kite or where. But since silk and bamboo were both available in China as early as 2000 B.C., it's possible that kites were flown there first. Kites probably spread to Korea and Japan and through Indo-China, Burma, Indonesia, Melanesia and Polynesia. Some kite-builders who lived on islands in the Pacific Ocean made their kites out of giant leaves.

Early kites were used for many purposes besides fun. In China, it was the custom to "kite away" the eldest son's bad luck on his seventh birthday. A birthday kite was flown and then released, supposedly taking the son's bad luck away with it. The bad luck was thought to go to the person who picked up the kite.

Kites were also used for sending messages or warning of danger. Small, agile kites were even used for sport fighting. In a fight, the object was to bring another kite down by smashing it or cutting its kite string. Sometimes kites were used in real battles too. Kites fitted with noisemakers or lights were flown over enemy camps at night to scare the enemy.

As the art of kite flying moved west, it lost some of its ceremonial and mystical aspects. Kites came to be thought of as toys or instruments for scientific experiments. Benjamin Franklin was extremely lucky that he wasn't killed when he flew a kite in a thunderstorm to see if lightning was electricity. Other experimenters tried flying kites to pull lifeboats and carriages, to hoist radio antennas and to observe the weather.

The kites that you'll make in this section are pure fun to make and to fly. You don't need any special equipment or kite materials, just ordinary stuff you can find in the kitchen.

The Garbage Bag Sled Kite

This kite is made out of simple materials, and it's easy to carry around because it can be folded up.

You'll need:
- a small, kitchen-sized plastic garbage bag
- four plastic drinking straws, each at least 22 cm (8½ inches) long
- light string
- tape
- scissors
- measuring tape or ruler

1 Cut the garbage bag as shown. It helps to draw the pattern on the bag with a felt pen first. Be sure to cut through both thicknesses of the bag. Do not cut along the bottom fold.

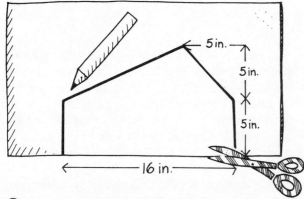

2 Open the kite and, if possible, tape it to a flat surface so that it doesn't slip around as you work on it.

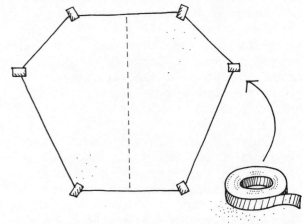

3 Join two straws together end to end so that you have one long straw. To do this, either pinch the end of one straw and insert it into the end of the other or tape the two straws end to end. Do the same with the other two straws.

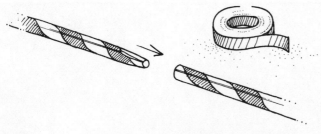

4 Tape the double-length straws to the kite as shown. If they're too long, cut off the ends.

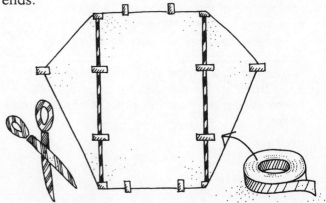

5 Remove the tape holding the kite down and turn the kite over. Reinforce the side points with tape so that they won't tear.

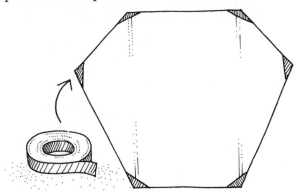

6 Add a string bridle that is 153 cm (60 inches) long. To do this, either punch a tiny hole and tie the bridle on or tape it on.

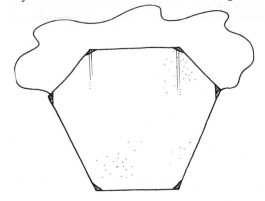

7 Find the centre of the bridle and tie a knot to form a loop. Tie a long flying string to this loop.

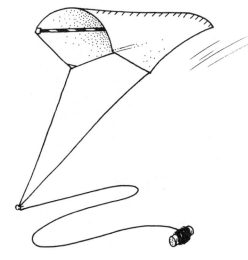

8 No trimming is needed for this kite. Just make sure the straws are underneath the kite when it is flying.

STRAWS UNDERNEATH.

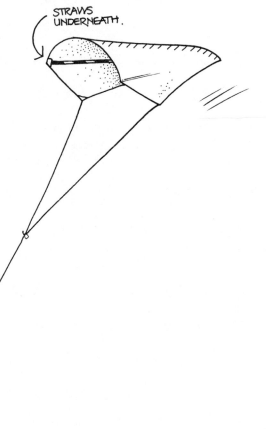

The Charinga

This folded paper kite with a tail flies beautifully in a light or moderate wind. A heavy wind will blow it inside out and make it difficult to fly.

You'll need:
- a sheet of foolscap or writing paper cut into a square
- paper that can be cut into long strips for a tail
- a strong thread
- sticky or masking tape
- scissors
- ruler

1 Fold the piece of paper in half, corner to corner.

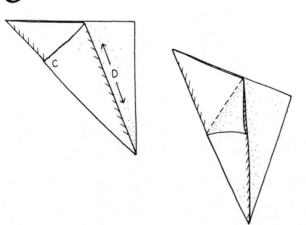

2 Fold point A over to edge B.

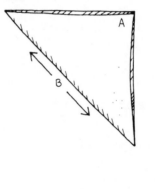
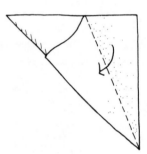

3 Fold point C over to fold D.

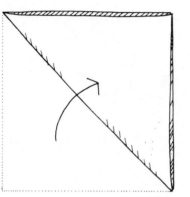

4 Turn the paper over and repeat steps 2 and 3 with the other side. Your kite should look like this:

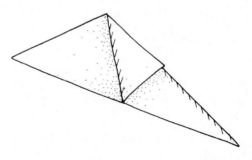

5 Cut off the top and bottom points as shown.

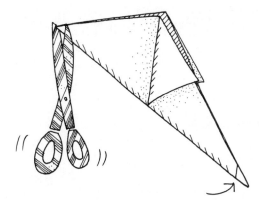

6 Unfold the kite and turn it so that the centre fold comes up towards you and the narrow end (the nose) is pointed away from you.

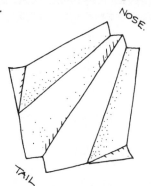

7 Cut a bridle out of strong thread. It should be long enough to go around the nose. Tape it to the kite as shown.

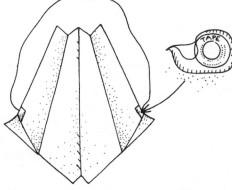

8 Find the centre of the bridle and tie a knot to form a loop. Tie a flying string to the loop on the bridle.

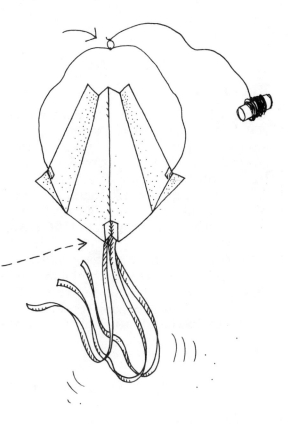

9 To make a tail for your kite, cut three strips of paper each 1 m (1 yard) long and 1 cm (½ inch) wide. Tape the strips to the tail of the kite.

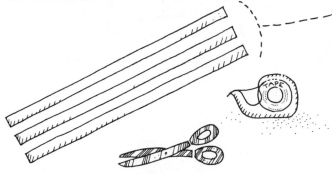

Trimming and Flying the Charinga

1 Be sure that the centre fold is pointed down when you fly the Charinga.

2 If the Charinga wobbles back and forth as it flies, add more tail. Take off some tail if the kite doesn't climb properly.

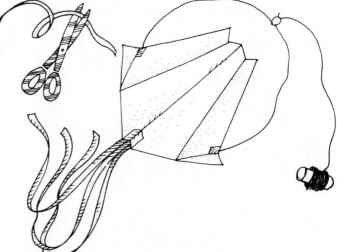

Kite-flying tips

There will be times when, no matter what you do, your kite flies badly, jerking around and perhaps even diving into the ground. When this happens, take a good look at where you're flying it. It could be that the wind is blowing around and over trees and buildings causing gusty air currents that are sending your kite all over the place.

The same problem can happen if the wind is blowing over the top of a hill and down a slope.

The very best kite flying condition is to have the wind blowing steadily up a gentle slope.

Learning from kites

Many aviation pioneers used kites in their pursuit of the secrets of flight. Sir George Cayley, who is considered to be the father of modern airplane flight, attached an arrow-like tail to a kite and made the world's first practical glider. The Wright brothers flew full-sized gliders as kites before climbing into them. Alexander Graham Bell in Canada and Samuel Cody in England both made man-carrying kites. Cody wanted to develop a way of lifting people into the air to observe battles.

1900
THE WRIGHT
BROTHERS.

CAYLEY'S GLIDER
1819.

The Bermuda Children's Kite

Some kites are so big that it takes teams of up to 20 people to fly them. This kite is so small you can fly it with two fingers.

You'll need:

- brown wrapping paper or a paper bag
- thin sticks (bamboo barbecue skewers work well, so do thin twigs and stir sticks)
- newspaper or tissue paper or crêpe paper for a tail, cut in strips 2 m (2 yards) long and 1.5 cm (¾ inch) wide
- thread
- scissors
- measuring tape or ruler

1 The pattern on page 75 is the actual size of the kite. Trace this pattern onto the brown paper.

2 Cut out the kite and punch small holes at the places shown.

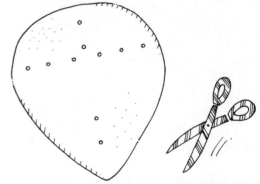

3 Cut the sticks to size and put them through the holes.

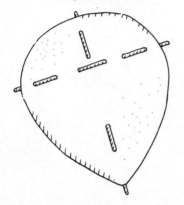

4 Cut a piece of thread about 25 cm (9¾ inches) long for the bridle. Attach it to the kite as shown.

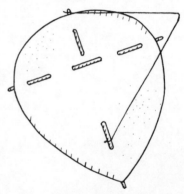

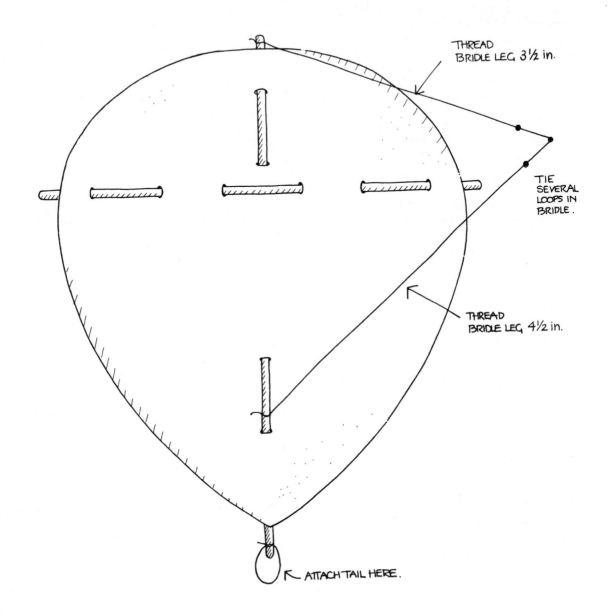

THREAD
BRIDLE LEG 3½ in.

TIE
SEVERAL
LOOPS IN
BRIDLE.

THREAD
BRIDLE LEG 4½ in.

ATTACH TAIL HERE.

5 Find the spot on the bridle where the distance to the top of the kite is about 9 cm (3½ inches) and the distance to the bottom of the kite is about 11.5 cm (4½ inches) Tie a small loop at this point.

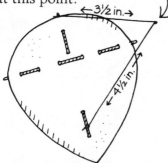

←3½ in.→

4½ in.

6 Tie small loops about 1 cm (½ inch) on each side of the first loop.

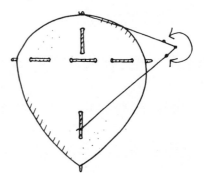

7 Tie a loop of thread to the bottom of the spar and tie or tape on the tail.

½ in. WIDE x 6 ft. LONG.

8 Tie the flying thread to the centre loop on the bridle. Turn to page 78 for trimming instructions.

Hold on!

Some kites can really pull on their strings. To save your hands and make the kite easier to hold, tie the end of the kite string around a tubular object such as a piece of broom handle, a cardboard tube, a plastic detergent bottle or even a tree branch.

Smart kite-flying rules

1. Do not fly near power lines. If your kite or the kite string comes into contact with a power line, let go immediately. Do not touch it again unless it falls completely clear of the power line. There is enough electricity in a power line to kill you instantly, so beware!

2. Don't fly if there is a thunderstorm nearby. Thunderstorms can also contain enough electricity to kill you. It is not a good idea to fly a kite in the rain or if the kite string gets wet.

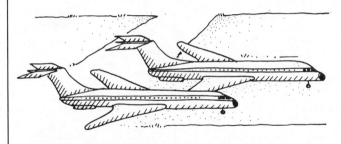

3. Do not fly near airports or any place where your kite could interfere with airplanes or gliders.

4. Do not fly over roads where your kite could interfere with road traffic.

5. Do not fly your kite over houses. If your kite crashes onto a house or flower garden, you will probably have some pretty angry people to deal with as well as a wrecked kite. I know this from personal experience. So steer clear.

6. Do not fly in crowds, where people could be hurt by the kite or cut by the kite string.
7. Do find a safe place and have fun.

Trimming and Flying the Bermuda Children's Kite

1 If the kite hangs back and will not climb, move the flying thread to the top loop of the bridle.

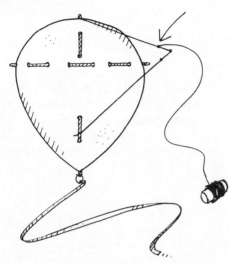

2 If the kite still hangs back, make another loop 1 cm (½ inch) farther towards the nose and tie on the flying thread. Continue making new loops and moving the flying thread until the kite flies well.

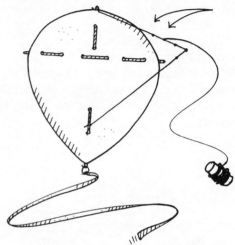

3 If moving the flying thread forward loop by loop doesn't work, the tail may be too heavy. Remove some of the tail and then start all over again, with the flying thread tied to the middle loop.

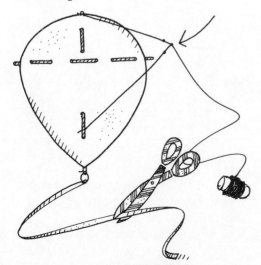

4 If the kite climbs too far overhead, move the flying thread one loop at a time towards the tail of the kite until the kite flies properly.

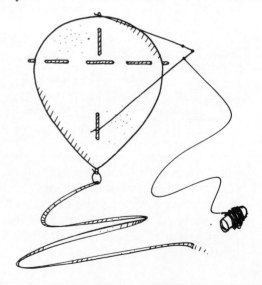

5 If the kites flies at a good height but darts from side to side, the tail may be too light. Add on to the tail until the kite flies well.

Changing where you tie the flying string onto the bridle changes the angle at which the kite meets the wind. The more the nose is pulled down (by tying the bridle towards the nose) the more the kite tends to fly up and overhead. The more the tail is pulled down (by tying the flying string towards the tail), the more the kite hangs back. Experiment to see what works best for your kite.

Some up-lifting info

When a kite flies, the same forces act on it as on an airplane or glider. (For more about these forces, see page 17.) Most of the lift on a kite comes from air pushing on the underside of the kite as it flies.

WIND DIRECTION (AIRFLOW)

If you liked **SUPER FLYERS**, you'll enjoy these fun kids' activity books by the Ontario Science Centre, the world-famous museum for active minds and bodies.

SCIENCEWORKS
65 Experiments That Introduce the Fun and Wonder of Science

The Ontario Science Centre
Illustrated by Tina Holdcroft

Did you know that you can actually hear through your teeth? That it's possible to make rain in your living room, and to see how fast the Earth is spinning? These are just a few of the sixty-five projects in this engaging book that will enable children to experience and enjoy science— as they're learning about it. "A collection of intriguing, easy experiments that are just plain fun as well as good basic science."
— The New York Times Book Review

$8.95   ISBN 0-201-16780-8

FOODWORKS
Over 100 Activities and Fascinating Facts That Explore the Magic of Food

The Ontario Science Centre
Illustrated by Linda Hendry

A delightful cornucopia of activities, games, and fascinating facts on the subject of food—from teeth, taste, and digestion to what's in it, who eats it, and how to make it. Kids will discover why they feel hungry and what happens to a hamburger after the first bite. They'll make ice cream without a machine and learn about food in space, desserts through history, the secret life of seeds, and much more. The quickest way to kids' minds is through their stomachs.

$7.95   ISBN 0-201-11470-4

▲
▼▼
Addison-Wesley Publishing Company, Inc.
Route 128
Reading, Massachusetts 01867